THOMAS CRANE PUBLIC LIBRARY

QUINCY MASS

CITY APPROPRIATION

RED-HOT BIKES
HONDA

Clive Gifford

SEA-TO-SEA

Mankato Collingwood London

This edition first published in 2009 by Sea-to-Sea Publications
Distributed by Black Rabbit Books
P.O. Box 3263
Mankato, Minnesota 56002

Printed in China

Library of Congress Cataloging-in-Publication Data:

Gifford, Clive.
  Honda / Clive Gifford.
     p. cm. – (Red-hot bikes)
  Summary: "Describes in detail the differences between 6 popular models of Honda
motorcycles, including statistics for each model and a brief history of the company Honda"--
Provided by publisher.
  Includes bibliographical references and index.
  ISBN 978-1-59771-136-4
  1. Honda motorcycle--Juvenile literature. I. Title.
  TL448.H6G52 2009
  629.227'5--dc22
                                          2008007315

9 8 7 6 5 4 3 2

Published by arrangement with the Watts Publishing Group Ltd, London.

Series editor: Adrian Cole
Series design: Big Blu
Art director: Jonathan Hair

Acknowledgments:

The Publisher would like to thank Honda UK

All images © Honda Motor Europe Limited

Every attempt has been made to clear copyright. Should there be any
inadvertent omission please apply to the publisher for rectification.

Contents

Honda—living the dream

Honda was formed in Japan in the 1940s by Mr. Soichiro Honda. Today, it makes more motorcycles every year than any other company. Honda began by making only motorcycles, but now also makes cars, speedboats, trucks, and many other power products.

Innovation

A major part of Honda's success has come from developing new ideas and working closely with customers. Honda has produced some motorcycle innovations, including the first bike with an automatic transmission, called the Hondamatic. In 2006, the company announced the first motorcycle airbag (see page 21).

Tech talk

Airbag—a safety device that inflates rapidly to help protect a rider if a crash occurs.

GP—short for Grand Prix, it is the top class of motorbike racing on a circuit.

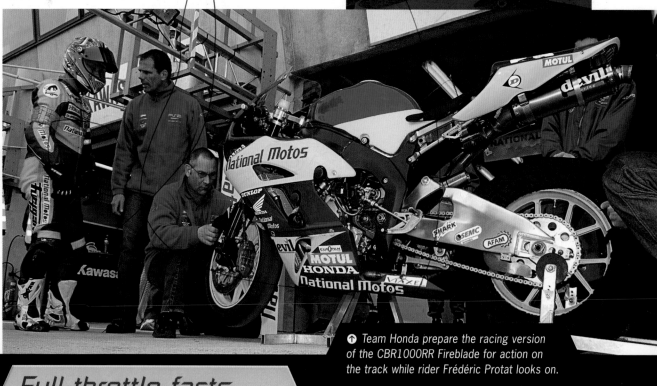

⬆ *Team Honda prepare the racing version of the CBR1000RR Fireblade for action on the track while rider Frédéric Protat looks on.*

Full throttle facts

Company name: Honda Motor Company Ltd.
Year of founding: 1948
First bike model: Dream D

Employees: almost 150,000
Headquarters: Tokyo, Japan
President: Mr. Takeo Fukui

Into racing

Soichiro Honda's childhood dream was to be motorcycle world champion, riding one of his own machines. Honda motorcycles have been involved in motor racing since the 1950s. They have won World Superbike and World GP500 championships, as well as off-road competitions such as the Baja 1000. Honda motorcycles have won the Baja 1000 a record 13 times and notched up 600 GP wins.

→ The all-new CBR1000RR Fireblade is a powerful road bike that has already tasted success in circuit racing, including TT Superbike and Le Mans 24-hour wins.

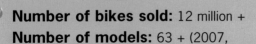

The Honda Ruckus was first released in the UK in 2005.

Current models

Today, Honda produces a wide range of motorcycles and motor scooters. These vary in size and speed from the small but nippy Ruckus scooter up to the large and powerful CBR1000RR. In this book you will get up close to six of Honda's most popular and exciting machines.

Number of bikes sold: 12 million +
Number of models: 63 + (2007, including scooters)

Best-selling model: CBR125R (2005)
Number of manufacturing plants: 120 (including cars and other vehicles)

Honda CB600F Hornet

Naked bikes are a special class of motorcycle. They are stripped of any fairing to give them a lean, mean street look. Naked bikes are designed for high performance and top speed. The Honda CB600F is also called the Hornet. It was first introduced in 1998. The Hornet was one of the first naked bikes. It is a fast, reliable machine that has helped to make naked bikes popular with riders, especially in Europe.

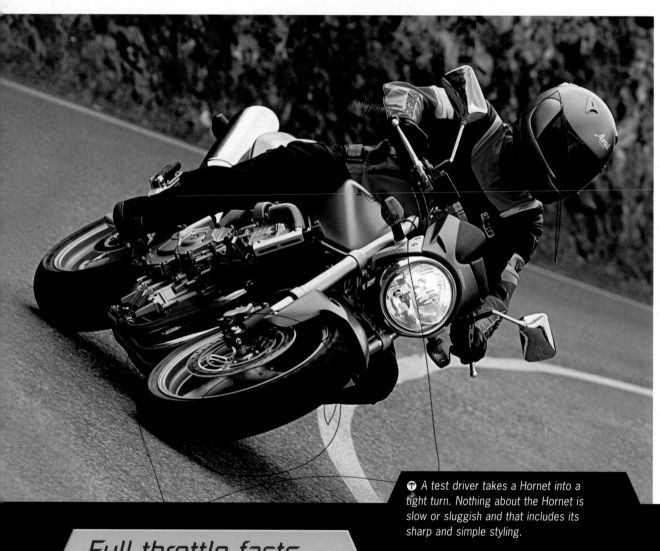

⬆ A test driver takes a Hornet into a tight turn. Nothing about the Hornet is slow or sluggish and that includes its sharp and simple styling.

Full throttle facts

Top speed: 140mph+ (225km/h+)
Length: 6ft 10in (2,090mm)

Ground clearance: 5in (135mm)
Fuel capacity: 5 gallons (19 liters)

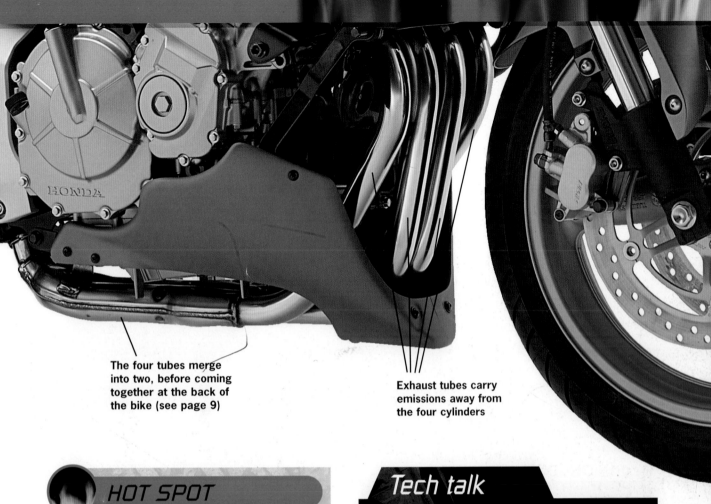

The four tubes merge into two, before coming together at the back of the bike (see page 9)

Exhaust tubes carry emissions away from the four cylinders

HOT SPOT

Exhausts

The Hornet has a 4-cylinder 36.6cu in (600cc) engine. The waste gases, called exhaust emissions, are carried out of each cylinder by an exhaust tube that merges first into two and finally one rear exhaust outlet on the right-hand side of the bike. This 4 into 2 into 1 exhaust system produces a throaty sound as the bike accelerates.

Tech talk

Accelerates—increases speed.

Fairing—a shell, usually made of plastic or fiberglass, fitted over the frame of some motorcycles to shield the rider and chassis from the wind.

Fuel capacity—the maximum amount of fuel that can be held by the petrol tank.

Curb weight—the total weight of a motorcycle with standard equipment and liquids including oil, coolant, and a full tank of fuel but not with a rider.

Curb weight: 436lb (198kg)
Seat height: 2ft 7in (800mm)

Engine capacity: 36.6cu in (600cc)
Transmission: 6 speed

Model development

The first major update of the Hornet came with the new model in 2000. Its front wheel was 1in (25mm) larger in diameter, its tail was shorter, and it featured better brakes. The next major update occurred in 2003 when the engine was retuned for more speed. The suspension was changed for a more stable ride. The 2003 model also featured: a 4.5 gallon (17-liter) fuel tank; a twin-bulb headlight; squared-up side mirrors instead of round ones and re-designed signal lights. In 2007 the Hornet featured an enlarged fuel tank and a redesigned instrument panel. It included a large tachometer dial and an electronic LCD display (see opposite page).

↟ The CB600F Hornet comes with a range of extra options. These include a small upper windshield known as a fly screen. Made of tinted plastic, it protects the rider's chest from wind blasts when the bike is powering along at high speed. Other options include an electric heater for the handlebar grips.

Honda CB600F

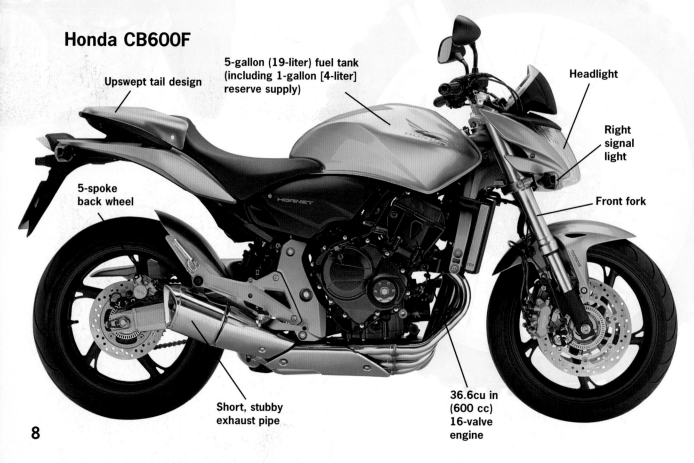

Upswept tail design

5-gallon (19-liter) fuel tank (including 1-gallon [4-liter] reserve supply)

Headlight

Right signal light

5-spoke back wheel

Front fork

Short, stubby exhaust pipe

36.6cu in (600 cc) 16-valve engine

HISS

HISS stands for Honda Ignition Security System. It was first fitted to a CB600F Hornet in 2003. HISS features a small electronic device inside the starter key known as a transponder. The ignition system will only turn on to start the engine if it detects the transponder in the key. Without it, the bike is immobilized, making it harder to steal.

↑ The Hornet's optional tankbag attaches to the fuel tank with magnets. It has a 3.4-gallon (13-liter) capacity and also contains a see-through map pocket and a built-in rain cover.

Squared-off side mirrors

Electronic LCD display

Tachometer dial

Throttle

Exhaust outlet

Drive chain

Tech talk

Immobilized—when a bike's engine is prevented from starting.

Tachometer—a device that measures the revolutions (revs) of a motorcycle engine and displays them to the rider.

Transponder—a wireless device which responds to a radio signal.

Honda CR85R

Motocross is an affordable motorsport that has more riders than any other form of motorcycle racing. The Honda CR85R is an entry-level machine for beginner and intermediate riders, but is packed with advanced features. It is used for motocross racing and general off-road riding over tough terrain.

⬆ A motocross rider puts a CR85R through its paces, plowing through a muddy turn, keeping the bike moving and his body balanced.

Full throttle facts

Top speed: 60mph (96km/h)
Length: 5ft 11in (1,803mm)

Ground clearance: 1ft 3in (311mm)
Fuel capacity: 1.4 gallons (5.3 liters)

Engine and drive train guard

Fold-up foot peg

⬆ *Foot pegs fold up when they are not needed and are cleated to offer excellent grip. A rider stands on them to lift up off the seat over large bumps.*

The bike wheel size

The CR85R comes in two versions with different wheel sizes. The CR85R has a 14in (355mm) back wheel and 17in (432mm) front wheel. The CR85R2 has a 19in (482mm) front wheel and 16in (406mm) rear.

Rider position

Off-road riding requires excellent balance. The CR85R has a long, slim, banana-shaped seat with a nonslip surface. This seat allows riders to move their body weight forward or backward from the handlebars. They do this to keep the bike under control up and down steep hills and drops.

Tech talk

Cleated—covered with studs to help grip.

Motocross—off-road race of around 40 riders over rough ground and jumps.

Curb weight: 165lb (75kg)
Seat height: 2ft 7in (824mm)

Engine capacity: 5.4cu in (85cc)
Transmission: 6 speed

Tough terrain

Motocross is an incredibly popular and exciting motorsport. Up to 40 riders start a race over a number of laps on an off-road circuit. The circuit contains challenges in the terrain including hills, ditches, and jumps. High-quality motocross bikes, such as the CR85R, have to be light, tough, and able to accelerate quickly at low speeds. They need only a small fuel tank, but must have hard, chunky tires with a deep tread pattern to grip the soft ground.

Ground clearance

Off-road and motocross riding often involves traveling over large bumps and obstacles, such as logs and boulders.

The CR85R has a high ground clearance of 1ft 3in (311mm) so it can be ridden over obstacles without damaging the bike.

HOT SPOT

Shock absorbers

Shock absorbers are air- or oil-filled cylinders connected to the wheel axles. The CR85R has very large shock absorbers that can travel, or move up and down, a long way. These cushion the impact of heavy landings. The CR85R's front shock absorber can travel up to almost 10in (245mm), and the rear up to 11in (275mm).

⊙ The CR85R has very simple controls that are all within easy reach so riders can concentrate on their path ahead. The levers and grips are adjustable for rider comfort.

Honda CR85R

Wide rear mudguard

Banana-shaped seat

Kickstart lever to start bike

Front mudguard

Aluminum rim wheels

Long travel suspension

High ground clearance

Lightweight liquid-cooled 5cu in (85cc) engine

Chunky-tread tires for maximum grip

Rear 7.4in (190mm) diameter disk brake

Front 8.6in (220mm) diameter disk brake

↑ A rider lifts up from the seat of his CR85R as he races off-road. He is wearing a motocross helmet, goggles, gloves, boots, and leathers.

Honda Shadow VT750C

Honda began selling the Shadow range of motorcycles in 1983. These cruiser-type machines have an upright riding style and widely spaced handlebars, making the bikes comfortable to ride over long distances. The latest Shadow, the VT750C, has lots of chrome detailing, a long wheelbase, and a V-twin engine.

⬆ A rider cruises down a dirt road onboard a brand new Honda Shadow 750. The rider sits upright with his feet positioned ahead of his body for a clear view of the road ahead.

Full throttle facts

Top speed: 100mph (160km/h)
Length: 8ft (2,505mm)

Ground clearance: 5in (130.8mm)
Fuel capacity: 3.7 gallons (14 liters)

Tech talk

Cylinders—the parts of the engine where fuel and air are ignited to produce power.

Detailing—when a small part of something is given special treatment.

Wheelbase—the distance from the rear axle to the front axle.

HOT SPOT

Engine configurations

Engine configuration usually means the number of cylinders an engine has and the pattern they are laid out in. The CBR1000RR Fireblade (see pages 26–29) has an inline 4 configuration, with four cylinders placed all in a straight row.

The Honda Shadow has a V-twin configuration. This means that the engine's two cylinders are placed at a V-shaped angle. In the Shadow VT750C's case the cylinders are angled 52 degrees apart.

⬆ *The Shadow VT750C's V-shaped engine is clearly visible in this photograph.*

Curb weight: 560.6lb (254.3kg)
Seat height: 2ft (658mm)

Engine capacity: 45.4cu in (745cc)
Transmission: 5 speed

The Shadow series

The Shadow series was introduced as a replacement for the older Honda Rebel. It was aimed at the U.S. bike market, where cruiser-type bikes are very popular. The first Shadow bikes were the VT500C and VT750C models. Over the years, the Shadow series has included small 7.6cu in (125cc) models, as well as the 2004 Shadow Sabre, which boasted a large 67cu in (1099cc) liquid-cooled engine.

In 2006, the model range reduced to just the Shadow VT750C—though the Shadow Spirit appeared in 2007. The VT740C can carry a load of up to 397lb (180kg). This is the equivalent of an adult rider and passenger, plus a full load in the saddlebags with weight to spare.

Luggage options

The Shadow VT750C luggage options:
- leather saddlebags
- a backrest bag
- a leather handlebar pouch
- a rear carrier
- a magnetic tankbag.

Tech talk

Clutch—the device that lets the rider select a gear.

Speedometer—displays the speed at which the bike is traveling.

Tripometer—a display of the distance traveled. This can be reset to zero by the rider.

The Honda Shadow VT750C has an unusually large speedometer mounted on top of the bike's 3.7-gallon (14-liter) fuel tank. It also includes a

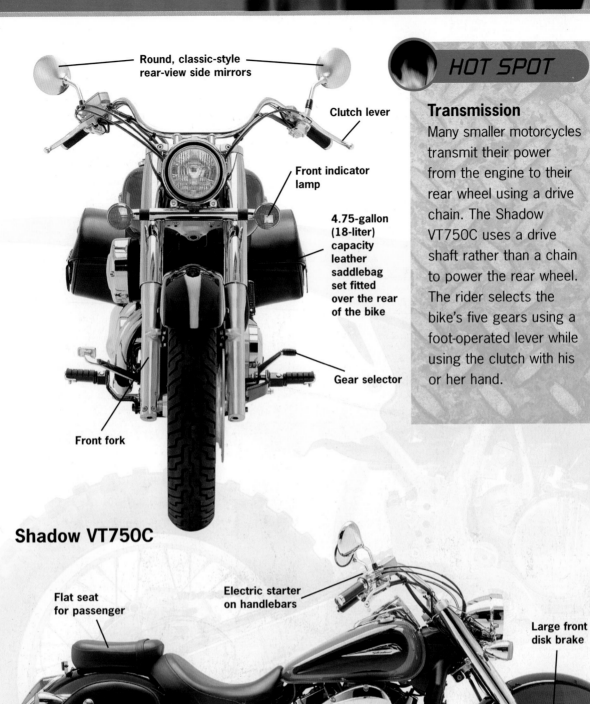

Round, classic-style rear-view side mirrors

Clutch lever

Front indicator lamp

4.75-gallon (18-liter) capacity leather saddlebag set fitted over the rear of the bike

Gear selector

Front fork

HOT SPOT

Transmission

Many smaller motorcycles transmit their power from the engine to their rear wheel using a drive chain. The Shadow VT750C uses a drive shaft rather than a chain to power the rear wheel. The rider selects the bike's five gears using a foot-operated lever while using the clutch with his or her hand.

Shadow VT750C

Flat seat for passenger

Electric starter on handlebars

Large front disk brake

Wheelbase measures 5ft 4in (1,639mm)

V-twin 45.5cu in (745cc) engine

Steel rimmed, wire-spoked wheels

Honda Gold Wing GL1800

The Honda Gold Wing is one of the most famous motorcycles models in the world. Thousands of riders and their passengers have enjoyed cruising over long distances on these powerful machines. The latest Gold Wing model, the GL1800, is the ultimate in motorcycle luxury. It has a powerful 80-watt sound system with six speakers, and a push-button electric reverse gear.

↑ The Honda Goldwing GL1800 is big enough for two people to travel comfortably over long distances.

Comfort package

The Gold Wing GL1800 comes with a comfort package for cold weather cruising. This includes electric handlebar grip heaters and a seat heater system for both the rider and passenger. Both functions are adjustable to six different temperature settings.

← This close-up of the GL1800's central console shows the ignition key and one of the seat heater setting dials.

Full throttle facts

Top speed: 130mph+ (210km/h+)
Length: 8ft 7in (2,635mm)

Ground clearance: 5in (125mm)
Fuel capacity: 6.6 gallons (25 liters)

HOT SPOT

Satellite navigation

The GL1800 comes with satellite navigation (sat nav). This system receives signals from satellites orbiting the Earth to help people work out their precise position when traveling around.

The Gold Wing's sat nav system is programmed with locations of Honda dealers and gas stations, and can be controlled using the rider's voice.

➋ The Gold Wing GL1800's high-tech control panel includes an intercom system, which enables the rider and passenger to speak to each other clearly.

Curb weight: 893lb (405kg)
Seat height: 2ft 5in (740mm)

Engine capacity: 112cu in (1832cc)
Transmission: 5 speed

Golden history

In 2005, the Gold Wing celebrated its 30th anniversary. The very first Gold Wing featured a 61cu in (999cc), 4-cylinder engine. In 1980 the first GL1100 model was sold, with a lockable trunk and a large fairing. In 1988, the bike grew in size again. The engine became a 6-cylinder, 92.7cu in (1520cc) beast and a reverse gear was added because of the machine's large size. The first GL1800 bike arrived in 2001. The 2006 version, fully loaded and fuelled, can weigh around 1,327lb (602kg), almost the same as a Formula One racing car.

Gold Wing GL1800 color options
- Black-Z
- Billet Silver Metallic
- Cabernet Red Metallic

Front speakers

Rear speakers

Honda Gold Wing GL1800

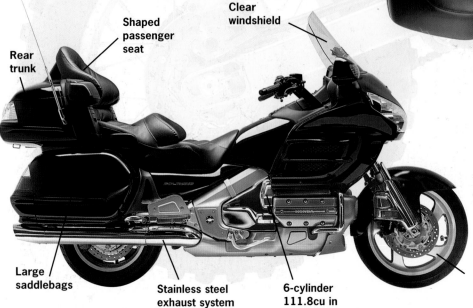

Rear trunk

Shaped passenger seat

Clear windshield

Large saddlebags

Stainless steel exhaust system

6-cylinder 111.8cu in (1,832cc) engine

Front 5-spoke wheel made of hollow cast aluminum

Motorbike airbag

The Gold Wing GL1800 is one of Honda's first bikes to have an airbag system installed to help protect the rider should there be a crash. Four sensors mounted on the front fork of the motorcycle send information about speed to the ECU (engine control unit). The ECU decides if a very sharp change in speed is a crash or just hard braking. If it thinks it is a crash, it triggers the airbag. This inflates to help protect the rider from a front impact.

Twin-beam dual headlights

Front double disk brake

Tech talk

ECU—short for engine control unit which is a computer that controls many of the engine's functions.

Formula One—the top class of specialized automobile racing on a circuit.

Inflates—to be blown up like a balloon.

Saddlebags—storage containers or boxes made to fit onto the sides of a bike.

Sensors—devices that measure something around them, such as speed or temperature.

Honda PS125i

Honda motorbikes first produced motor scooters with small engines for the Japanese market. Today, scooters are a popular alternative to cars for commuters all over the world. They cost far less to buy and maintain. The PS125i motor scooter was introduced in 2006. It has a steel frame with a fuel-injected, liquid-cooled 7.6cu in (125cc) engine. Its sister model, the PS150i, has a slightly larger engine.

⬆ One option for the PS125i is a rugged windshield made of a tough plastic called polycarbonate. The windshield includes knuckle visors to shield the rider's hands.

⬆ The PS125i's 7.6cu in (125cc) engine provides enough power to allow two people to ride comfortably on the scooter's long seat.

Full throttle facts

Top speed: 50mph (80km/h)
Length: 6ft 6in (1,990mm)

Ground clearance: 5in (125mm)
Fuel capacity: 2 gallons (8 liters)

Engine and emissions

The PS125i's 4-stroke engine is very economical, which means it uses less fuel over a longer distance. The scooter is also one of the cleanest bikes around. It uses an advanced control system and produces very low emissions from its exhaust.

Color options

• Max Gray Metallic (with Fury Red)
• Interstellar Black Metallic (with Ardesia Gray)
• Winter Lake Blue Metallic (with Ardesia Gray)
• Candy Xenon Blue (with Ardesia Gray)

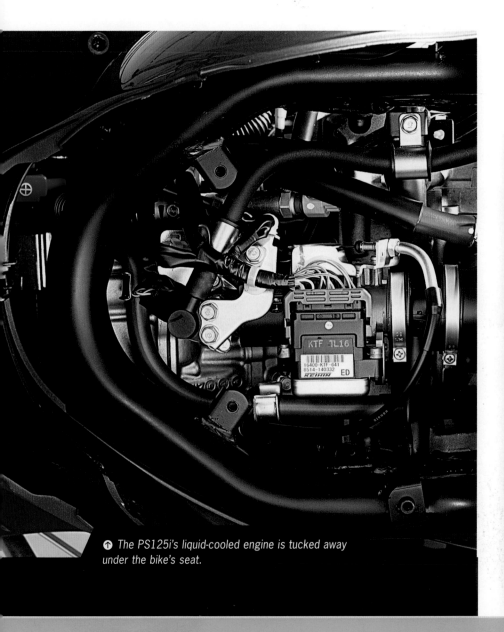

↑ *The PS125i's liquid-cooled engine is tucked away under the bike's seat.*

Tech talk

Emissions—the harmful gases released from a motor vehicle's exhaust into the atmosphere.

Fuel injection—a system that carefully controls the amount of fuel entering an engine cylinder.

Motor scooter—a small motorcycle with a step-through frame, usually with an engine size of between 3cu in (50cc) and 24.4cu in (400cc).

Curb weight: 278lb (126kg)
Seat height: 2ft 7in (800mm)

Engine capacity: 7.6cu in (125cc)
Transmission: automatic

Riding position

The PS125i has been carefully designed to give a comfortable, upright riding position. It has a higher driving position than many scooters, with the seat 2ft 7in (800mm) from the ground. This gives the rider a good view of the road and traffic. It has a large, flat footboard, allowing riders to place their feet in many different positions. The side bodywork narrows in the middle of the scooter to allow the feet to reach the ground easily.

Honda PS125i

55–60-watt front headlight

Brake levers

Front signal lights

Air inlets to cool radiator

Brake light

Rear wheel mudguard

Seat height 2ft 7in (800mm) from ground

Throttle

Fold-up bike stand

Footboard

6-spoke wheels made from cast aluminum

Brakes

The PS125i has a combined brake system. The right-side brake lever controls the front brake, an 8.6in (220mm) disk brake. The left lever operates both the front brake and the 5in (130mm) rear drum brake. This makes it easier for beginners to control the scooter while gripping the throttle.

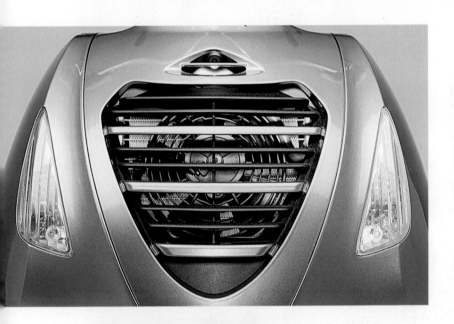

Cool down

The PS125i's engine radiator is built into the scooter's nose. The air inlets (left) are positioned directly below the headlight, between the front indicator lamps. They help the radiator to receive a blast of air when powering forward. The radiator keeps the engine cool and running at its ideal temperature.

Tech talk

Disk brake—a brake system where brake pads press onto a disk attached to the motorcycle wheel. This action slows the bike down and stops the wheel from turning.

Drum brake—a brake system where a set of brake pads press against a cylinder attached to the motorcycle wheel. It works in the same way as a disk brake.

Radiator—a water-filled cooling system that lowers the temperature of the engine and stops it from overheating. Fan-assisted radiators are also blasted by an electric fan.

Honda CBR1000RR Fireblade

Back in 1992, Honda released their first Fireblade motorcycle; the CBR900RR. It was designed by Mr. Tadao Baba. It aimed to have the power and raw speed of a larger bike, equipped with a 55cu in (900cc) engine, but turn and handle like a much smaller machine.

At the time the Fireblade revolutionized fast, powerful supersport bikes. It was a lot lighter and more agile than any of its rivals. The latest Fireblade model, the CBR1000RR, continues the trend.

↑ *Sleek lines, very high power and, low weight add up to make the CBR1000RR Fireblade a top performer both on the road and in track-based racing competitions.*

Full throttle facts

Top speed: 160mph+ (260 km/h+)
Length: 6ft 7in (2,030mm)

Ground clearance: 5in (130mm)
Fuel capacity: 4.75 gallons (18 liters)

Red hot racer

The 2006 Fireblade's engine is tuned to perform well at high speeds. Its maximum torque level is 10,000 rpm, whereas the previous model peaked at 8,500 rpm. The motorcycle can accelerate from a standing start to 60mph (100km/h) in less than three seconds.

➔ *The Fireblade's instrument panel features a digital speedometer and a large tachometer dial with its redline starting at 12,500 rpm.*

Tech talk

Redline—maximum safe engine speed for a motorbike. It is often shown on a tachometer dial in red.

Rpm—short for revolutions per minute; a measurement of the speed of a motorbike's engine.

Torque—the force produced by an engine to move the drive chain, which powers the rear wheel of the motorcycle.

⬆ *This protective cover is specially made to fit the Honda Fireblade.*

Curb weight: 447.5lb (203 kg)
Seat height: 2ft 8in (831mm)

Engine capacity: 60.9cu in (998cc)
Transmission: 6 speed

Input from racing

From 2004 onward, the Fireblade models were designed and built using input from Honda's successful MotoGP racing team. Their experience and technology helped produce better bikes. The latest Fireblade features a lightweight aluminum frame and a weight-forward design. This means the bike can get more power to the ground quicker when coming out of corners.

Honda CBR 1000RR

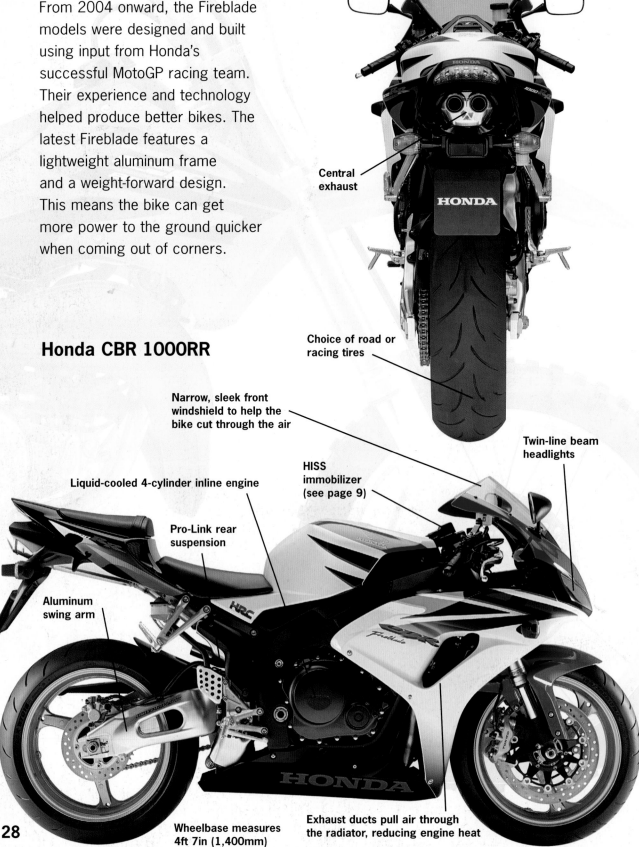

Central exhaust

Choice of road or racing tires

Narrow, sleek front windshield to help the bike cut through the air

Twin-line beam headlights

Liquid-cooled 4-cylinder inline engine

HISS immobilizer (see page 9)

Pro-Link rear suspension

Aluminum swing arm

Wheelbase measures 4ft 7in (1,400mm)

Exhaust ducts pull air through the radiator, reducing engine heat

28

Le Mans Moto

The Le Mans 24 Hours is one of the most famous car races in the world. A version is also held for motorcycles, the 24 Hours Moto. It is an awesome test of both the riders and their bikes' speed, stamina, and reliability. The 2006 race was won by a Honda Fireblade, which notched up more than 800 laps in the 24 hours of continuous racing.

Tech talk

MotoGP—a top competition in motorcycle circuit racing.

Swing arm—the movable joint between the motorcycle frame and the rear axle. It supports the rear wheel and its suspension parts.

The No.55 Honda Fireblade, ridden over 24 hours by a team of three riders: Dani Ribalta, Olivier Four, and Frédéric Protat, on its way to winning the 2006 Le Mans 24 Hours Moto, two laps ahead of its nearest rival.

Glossary

Axle—the central shaft that a wheel spins around.

Cruiser—a motorcycle, usually with a small fuel tank, an upright riding style, and feet-forward seating.

cu in—short for cubic inches, it is used as a measurement of the size of the engine's cylinders (cc is short for cubic centimeters).

Drive chain—similar to a bicycle chain, this is a chain that transmits power from the engine to the rear wheel.

Foot pegs—rests or short poles that stick out from the sides of the bike and give riders somewhere to place their feet.

Grip—the ability of a vehicle to stay connected to the ground. Also refers to the ends of the handlebars that the rider holds.

Handling—the way a motorcycle responds when being ridden, such as how it turns into and out of corners.

Horsepower (hp)—a unit of measurement used for giving the amount of power an engine generates.

Kickstart lever—a foot pedal used to start the engine of some motorcycles. Other motorbikes have an electric starter.

mph—miles per hour; a measurement of speed (km/h is short for kilometers per hour).

Saddlebags—containers that hang over the sides of the bike behind the rider.

Shock absorbers—devices that are designed to absorb sudden forces and impacts to the suspension of the vehicle.

Suspension—the system of springs, shock absorbers, and other components, directly connected to the wheels or the axles to help create a smooth ride. Changes to suspension levels affect the handling of a race vehicle.

Swing arm—a movable joint between the frame of the motorcycle and the rear axle.

Tachometer—a dial or display that tells the rider the speed of the engine in revolutions per minute (rpm).

Throttle—a device that controls the flow of fuel to an engine—the faster the flow, the higher the speed.

Wheelbase—the distance between the front and rear axles of a vehicle.

Further information

Web sites

http://powersports.honda.com/
The official US web site of Honda. This web site is full of pictures and details of Honda's latest bikes.

http://motorcycles.about.com/od/hondaother/
A handy list of links to other Honda web sites, produced by the About.com network.

http://www.bikez.com/brand/honda_motorcycles.php
An enormous list of major Honda motorcycle models from the 1970s to the present day. Click on a link to learn more about each bike including its specifications.

http://www.ama-cycle.org/
Founded in 1924, the AMA protects and promotes the interests of the world's largest and most dedicated group of motorcycle enthusiasts. The AMA focuses on rights, riding and racing.

Books

The Honda Story
Ian Falloon (Haynes Group, 2005).
An in-depth guide to Honda's road and racing motorcycles from the 1940s to the present day.

Honda Gold Wing: The Complete Story
Phil West (The Crowood Press, 2003).
A detailed account of Honda's most famous cruising bike from its launch in the 1970s.

Honda Motorcycles: The Ultimate Guide
Doug Mitchel (Krause Publications, 2005).
A photo-packed look at Honda's motorcycles through the decades.

Honda Motorcycles
Aaron Frank (Motorbooks International, 2003).
A great guide to the history of Honda and its leading motorcycles.

Honda timeline

1948—Honda Motor Co. Ltd. is founded in Japan.

1949—Honda's first motorcycle, the 6cu in (98cc) Dream D, is produced.

1959—Honda makes its first appearance in motorcycle racing at the Isle of Man TT.

1963—Honda opens its first overseas factory in Belgium.

1973—Company founder, Mr. Soichiro Honda, retires.

1974—The first Honda Gold Wing, the GL1000, is put on sale in the United States.

1976—Honda produces its first motorcycle with automatic transmission, the CB750A Hondamatic.

1983—Honda introduces its first version of the Shadow.

1985—A major new Honda Gold Wing, the GL1500, is produced.

1992—Honda produce their first Fireblade, the CBR900RR.

1998—The first Honda CB600 Hornet is produced, sparking interest in naked bikes.

2005—Honda produces its 150 millionth motorcycle. Honda records its 600th win in World championship Grand Prix racing, more than any other manufacturer.

2006—An exciting new supersports bike, CBR1000RR FireBlade, is released.

Index

DATE DUE

Central Children's

OCT 2008